Stories
from
Our
Living
Past

by FRANCINE PROSE

edited by JULES HARLOW

ASSOCIATE EDITOR
Seymour Rossel

Illustrated by Erika Weihs

Stories from Our Living Past

BEHRMAN HOUSE, INC. Publishers
New York, N.Y.

For Parents and Teachers

To a greater or lesser degree, every civilization idealizes its past. In our own country, for example, children learn in school of a republic established by men imbued with the highest moral purpose and bent upon giving universal social and political form to an abstract principle of individual liberty; or of a civil war waged nobly by two foes, the one struggling to vindicate a principle of human equality, the other to defend a proud and cultivated way of life. These visions of history, which are essentially mythological in nature, contain a large measure of distortion, but an equally large measure of truth: ideal truth. Viewed through the lens of mythology, the actual events and figures of history assume inflated proportions; as if at the necessary bidding of society itself, they undergo a crucial and far-ranging fictionalization. Men in the mythic vision become heroes, perfect and whole in their character, altogether consistent in behavior—and in nothing more consistent or more perfect than in their unyielding devotion to inflexible principle. Events themselves, shedding the skin of circumstance and accident, stand forth in their boldest and most compelling aspect: they become turning points, inevitable, unique, laden with significance, prefigurative of the future course of history. But if inflation is one characteristic of the mythologizing impulse, simplification is another. The great myths and legends do not on the whole concern themselves with complexities of human motivation —with the shades and nuances of individual personality, the subtle maneuvers of the spirit and the discriminating actions of consciousness. They tell a simple, if grandiose, tale.

Mythology, then, is the conscious effort to recreate the past as a model, and a civilization stamps itself uniquely and for all time in accordance with the particular models it chooses to enshrine and celebrate in its legends. In the mythological literature of the West, the models settled upon have frequently been the fixed virtues of character, as in the great epic poems that strive to illustrate, through the dramatic tale of a hero's adventures, those qualities which the culture holds most dear: the cunning of Odysseus, for instance, or the fortitude of Aeneas, the constancy of Lancelot or the valor of Roland at Roncevaux. In each case the quality is regarded as inseparable from the legendary hero who embodies and exemplifies it and whose character, considerably larger than life, dominates the epic narrative as a whole. The hero and the virtue he typifies, one and inseparable, constitute the mythic model.

In several critical respects the models offered by the myths and legends of the Jewish people differ from this norm, and the differences themselves tell us much about the specific values of Judaism. Rather than as figures of superhuman proportions, the principals of Jewish legend—even of those legends based directly on the heroic narratives of the Bible—appear to us in the common garb of humanity; whereas the epic hero is larger than life, the "hero" of Jewish legend is precisely life-sized. Furthermore, what the typical Jewish legend strives to inculcate is not a specific trait of character, an inner disposition or abstract virtue, but rather a pattern of ideal human behavior; emphasis is laid on strategies of action rather than on the cultivation of a given quality of spirit. At the heart of these divergencies, as we might expect, lies a distinction of value. The moral world of the epic poem is self-contained and self-referring. It is the hero alone who defines the behavior which marks him, in turn, as a human paragon; apart from him, the model does not exist. Jewish myth, by contrast, insists on a standard of judgment beyond the narrative frame, in the body of revealed truth that is the law and faith of Israel; the model exists only with reference to that standard. While the epic encourages us to identify spiritual excellence with a particular figure and with the heroic qualities he displays, Jewish legend encourages us to recognize and esteem those elements of behavior that most closely resemble the ideals embodied in Jewish law; to this exercise considerations of person and of attitude are finally irrelevant.

Such differences aside, however, all myth may be said to share a common purpose. In offering an idealized version of the past, accompanied often enough by a large measure of the wishful and the imaginary, by improbable juxtapositions of time and place and by fanciful characterization, it conveys a species of truth which no "objective" account of reality can match. Mythological truth is not the same as historical truth, which is infinitely more complicated and brutal. Nor is it the same as abstract truth, the truth of philosophy and of religion. Mythology tells us the truth about ourselves by reminding us of the moral possibilities of our own lives, and it does so by giving us the events and figures of our past as models of perfection. Its truth is injunctive, holding out the hope of moral advancement, and investing us with the urge to create a future worthy of such models, of such a past.

J. H.
New York City
Tammuz 5732

Contents

UNIT II *Self-Respect Is Holy*

UNIT III *Love of Neighbor — Justice, Mercy, Compassion — Is Holy*

UNIT IV *Our Responsibilities*

1 The Binding of Isaac

Introduction

Abraham lived long, long ago. In his time most men worshiped many false "gods," and the way they worshiped was often cruel. But Abraham and his wife Sarah and their son Isaac worshiped only the One God. And they knew God loved His people. The Jewish faith began with Abraham and his family.

Story

God commanded Abraham to take his son Isaac to the land of Moriah, and to sacrifice him as an offering to the Lord.

Abraham loved his son dearly, but he trusted God and obeyed God's will.

So he called his son, and two servants, and set off toward the hills of Moriah.

When they reached the base of the hills, Abraham ordered his servants to remain behind. Then, holding Isaac's hand in his, he began to climb the mountain.

Abraham and Isaac climbed for several hours until they were near exhaustion. Then they rested.

"Father," said Isaac. "I see that you have the knife and the firewood to make the burnt offering. But tell me: Where is the lamb for us to sacrifice to God?"

"God will provide the lamb," replied Abraham.

Abraham's voice sounded strange which troubled his son. But Isaac trusted his father, and so they continued up the mountain.

When they reached the top, Isaac knew there **was something** wrong—there was no lamb in **sight**. The air was cool and quiet. Dark clouds **rushed** across the sky. And Abraham's cheeks **were** covered with tears.

At that moment, Isaac understood. *He* would **be** Abraham's offering to God.

Isaac stood very still. He could not speak. **Abraham** bound him with rope and set him upon **the altar.**

Abraham raised the knife.

Suddenly Abraham heard a voice calling to him from heaven. He began to tremble, and the **knife** fell to the ground.

"Abraham!" cried the voice of God. "Behind you, in the thicket, is a ram. That ram shall be your offering to the Lord. Your son Isaac shall live.

"You are a righteous man, Abraham. You did as I commanded, even though it might have meant the death of your beloved son. Because of that, I shall reward you. Your descendants shall be as numerous as the stars in the sky. And I shall bless you and your people."

After the voice of God grew still, the air became quiet again. Abraham and Isaac sacrificed the ram.

Questions

1 If Abraham loved Isaac, why did he prepare to sacrifice him?

2 Did God indeed demand the sacrifice of Isaac?

3 What do you think God did actually want of Abraham?

15

Daniel in the Lions' Den

2

Introduction

Daniel was a trusted servant of the king and held a high position at court. But the king he served was a Persian king, not a Jew. By the time of Daniel, the Jewish people were scattered in many lands. The stories of Daniel are stories of the Exile. See what this one has to say.

Story

When Darius became King of Persia, he chose Daniel as his closest advisor. He trusted Daniel more than any man in the kingdom.

The princes of Darius' court were jealous of Daniel. Yet they could not find a way to make the king stop trusting him.

One day, as the princes watched Daniel saying his prayers, one of them had an idea. He waited until evening, when the king was sleepy from food and wine. Then the prince began his evil plan.

"Your Majesty," he said, "do you think it is right that your subjects should bow down to anyone but you?"

"No," replied the king, "it is not."

"Then let us make a new law," said the prince. "Let us make it illegal to bow down to any man or god besides yourself. And let us punish the wrongdoers by throwing them into a den of hungry lions."

"Very well," said King Darius, yawning sleepily. And he placed his royal stamp on the new law.

The next morning all the princes approached Darius' throne. "Your Majesty," said one, "your new law has already been broken."

"Who dares do such a thing?" demanded the king.

"It is Daniel," replied another of the princes with a sly smile. "He bows down and prays to his God three times a day."

"But Daniel is my most trusted advisor," said the unhappy king.

"Still, he must be thrown into the lions' den," insisted the princes. "It is the king's new law!"

Although Darius loved Daniel, he knew that he had no choice. That night Darius led Daniel to the cave. When the king heard the lions' roars, he could hardly keep from trembling.

17

"Pray to your God, Daniel," he said. "Perhaps He will deliver you from this terrible fate."

Then Daniel walked into the lions' den.

All that night the princes drank wine, and celebrated their victory. All that night the king lay awake in his bed, and worried about Daniel.

The next morning King Darius returned to the cave. And behold, an amazing sight! When the rock covering the cave's mouth was rolled away, Daniel came forth from the lions' den.

"Daniel!" cried the king. "How were you saved from the lions?"

"Last night," replied Daniel, "as I walked into the dark cave, I began praying to God. Suddenly the lions grew very quiet, as if they were listening. One by one, they shut their fierce jaws. One by one, they lay down at my feet, and drifted off to sleep."

Darius and Daniel hugged each other joyously. Then the king ordered the evil princes to be punished in the lions' den.

And so King Darius came to love the God of Israel, who had answered Daniel's prayers, and delivered Daniel from the lions' den.

Questions

1   What new Persian law did Daniel break?

2   What great commandment of God was Daniel determined to keep?

3   How do you think Daniel's innocence and his trust in God helped preserve his life? Did God help Daniel?

The Lie Takes a Partner

Introduction

Can you see a lie? Draw a picture of it? Poke it in the ribs? Of course not! But you know it can do a lot of harm. In this story the lie is per-son-i-fied—written about as though it were a living person. So is Wickedness. See how they work together.

Story

Long ago God commanded Noah to build an ark.

"Soon," said God, "I will send down a flood to wash away the evil in the world. But, because you are a good man, I have chosen you and your family to begin life again, after the flood is over.

"Go now and build an ark. Then bring in two of every kind — one male and one female — so that each pair will be able to start a family when the earth is dry again."

So Noah did as God commanded. Each day, as the sky drew darker and storm clouds grew blacker, Noah loaded the ark with animals. Lions roared. Dogs barked. Cows mooed. Giraffes lowered their long necks to pass beneath the doorways. Truth came in, together with Peace. Love came in, holding Good Deeds by the hand. All came in pairs, two by two, just as the Lord had ordered.

And rain began to trickle from the sky.

One day, as the waters were beginning to rise, a small, thin figure, completely covered by a long, hooded, black cloak, tried to sneak onto the ark past Noah.

"Stop!" cried Noah. "I know who you are!" "You are the Lie! And you cannot board my ark alone, because the Lord has commanded that every creature must have a partner."

"But I *do* have a partner!" lied the Lie. "She is coming later."

"I know your tricks," answered Noah. "You cannot fool me. Go away, and do not return unless you can find a mate."

Now the Lie knew that the flood was very near; he had no time to lose. He began to run wildly through the countryside, asking everyone he met to be his partner. But the Lie was such a mean, ugly little fellow that no one would agree.

At last, in the middle of a dark, gloomy forest, the Lie saw a toothless old hag. Her face was wrinkled, her hair long and tangled. She was pulling the wings off beautiful butterflies, and laughing as they fell helplessly to the ground.

"Who are you?" asked the Lie.

"I am Wickedness," she replied.

"I love you!" cried the Lie. "Marry me and go with me to Noah's ark. A terrible flood is coming and the Lord has commanded that no one can be saved without a partner!"

"You are the Lie," said Wickedness. "How do I know you are telling the truth?"

"I promise you," said the Lie. "This time, I am not lying. And, just to prove it, I will do anything. If you will only come with me, I will do anything you ask."

Wickedness thought for a long time. Then she turned to the Lie with a toothless grin.

"I will make you a bargain," she said. "I will be your partner on the ark. But, in return, you must give me everything you gain by lying, from this day on, and forever."

"That is a high price to pay," sighed the Lie. "But I have no choice. I must agree. Now let us go quickly, and make our way quietly onto the ark. I am afraid that Noah does not like us, and may try to give us trouble."

That night, when the thunder and lightning had already begun, and the animals were bellowing and roaring with fear, Wickedness and the Lie walked onto the ark.

Noah frowned when he saw them. But the Lie had found a partner, and so he was allowed to come on board.

And so it happened that evil and dishonesty remained in the world, even after the flood was over and the sky was blue and clear again. Ever since Wickedness has held the Lie to the terms of their bargain, so that everything gained by lying has helped Wickedness grow healthy and strong.

And their partnership has continued to this very day.

Questions

1 Which of the Ten Commandments forbids us to lie about others?

2 What comes from lying?

3 What feelings in people cause them to lie? to tell the truth?

4

The Sabbath Spice

Introduction

"If I were king . . ." That's a fine wish! If we were kings we could have anything we wanted—almost anything, couldn't we? The emperor Antoninus could always have anything he wanted—most especially anything to eat. But one spice was different from all the others . . .

Story

One night the Roman emperor Antoninus was invited by Rabbi Judah to dinner. The two men were good friends.

The emperor was a huge, fat man, who loved good food as much as anything in his empire. And so the Rabbi's cook prepared a wonderful feast, with hundreds of different dishes, all steaming hot, fresh, and fragrant.

First the emperor drank ten bowls of delicately-spiced soup. Then he ate a whole roast kid, five tender chickens, and a triple helping of wild rice. At last, when his stomach was so full that it rubbed against the edge of the table, he pushed away his plate.

"Thank you for this excellent dinner."

"You must come again on the Sabbath," replied Rabbi Judah.

A few days later, on a Friday evening, the emperor came again to Rabbi Judah's house. Because of God's commandment to rest on the Sabbath, the rabbi's cook could not work in the kitchen that night, so she prepared all the food earlier in the afternoon.

The meal was very simple. There was a platter of roast meat, a bowl of vegetables, and a loaf of bread.

For just an instant, the emperor frowned with disappointment. But, as he tasted the food, he began to rub his stomach happily.

"This food is extraordinary!" he cried. "Please Rabbi, tell me what secret spice your cook uses to make these simple dishes taste so delicious!"

"It is a spice called the Sabbath," replied Judah.

"Then I must have some for the royal kitchen," said emperor Antoninus. "Please, give me a pinch of the Sabbath spice, so I can teach my cook to use it."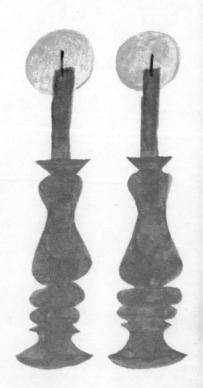

"I am sorry," smiled the rabbi, "but this spice cannot be given away. Whether or not you have it depends on you.

"For you see, Your Majesty, the delicious flavor of this meal comes from the delight we take in keeping the Sabbath."

Questions

1 Have you ever eaten a truly simple meal and enjoyed it very much? Why was that?

2 What is it, do you think, that makes the Sabbath meal special?

3 List the things you think make up the spice called Sabbath.

The Two Jewels

5

Introduction

We may like many beautiful and precious things in the world. But what about the people who are close and dear to us? We love them and we value them beyond mere things. And it sometimes comes about that we need to remember— and remember very well—that over and above all is God, the One God who treasures each of us.

Story

One Sabbath afternoon, Rabbi Meir's two ailing sons suddenly died. Lovingly the rabbi's wife, Beruriah, kissed them goodbye. Then she began to worry: How could she tell her husband such terrible news on the Sabbath?

The Sabbath is a day of peace and of rest. Nothing evil should be uttered on the holy day. So she quietly closed the door to the boys' room, and went into the parlor to await the rabbi's return from the synagogue.

28

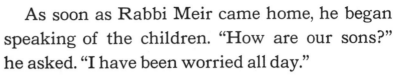

As soon as Rabbi Meir came home, he began speaking of the children. "How are our sons?" he asked. "I have been worried all day."

"They are resting peacefully now," said Beruriah. "We should not disturb them." And, before her husband could ask any more questions, she began to serve the Sabbath meal.

Taking her at her word, the rabbi sat down to eat. But, as evening drew near, and not one sound came from the boys' room, he grew alarmed.

"Perhaps the children are thirsty," he said. "I will go see if they need anything." He got up from his chair, and headed toward the bedroom.

"Wait!" Beruriah cried so loudly that her startled husband stopped in his tracks. "I have a problem and need your advice."

"Listen," she began, drawing him near. "Long ago, a man from my father's village entrusted me with two fine jewels, a diamond and a ruby. He told me to keep them until he wanted them back. This very afternoon, he appeared at our door, asking for his jewels. Do you think I should return them?"

"Of course," replied Rabbi Meir, surprised that she had never mentioned these jewels before. "You should return them at once and thank the man for letting you enjoy them for so long."

29

"Those jewels were our sons," explained Beruriah. "They were entrusted to us by God. This afternoon, the Lord came to claim them."

In this way, Rabbi Meir's wife helped her husband to accept the death of their sons without bitterness.

Questions

1 To what precious jewels did the rabbi's wife compare her children?

2 How did Beruriah's respect for the Sabbath help her to control her grief when the children died?

3 How did her love and reverence for God help her comfort her husband?

6   The Legend of the Honey

Introduction

Did you ever have a hard time trying to decide what to give someone for a present, for his birthday, perhaps, or for Hanukkah? The angels once had to decide on a gift for someone special. They made a good choice, as you will see—a very Jewish choice.

Story

Once there lived a grocer named Simon ben Yehuda. He was a small, thin man, with a bald spot on top of his head. He was not very rich, or very clever. On the surface, Simon was a very ordinary man.

But his heart was extraordinarily good. He was kind, forgiving, and modest. Whenever a poor man came into his shop, Simon ben Yehuda gladly gave him the choicest fruits and vegetables.

One day, an angel, disguised as a ragged beggar, visited the grocer's store. Before the angel could speak one word, Simon loaded his arms full of apples, raisins, and carrots.

So the angel told the other angels that Simon ben Yehuda should be rewarded for his good heart. But the grocer already had enough money, a loving wife, and a wonderful son. He was happy. What else could they give him?

For seven days and seven nights, all the angels in heaven debated that question. Then they had an idea.

Why not make his son love learning, they decided. Surely that would bring Simon joy.

So the angels went to the far corners of the world, to gather the rarest, purest, sweetest honey on earth and then the angels waited.

At last the day arrived. For the first time, Simon brought his son to the classroom. For the first time, the boy opened the pages of his schoolbooks.

Suddenly the whole school was filled with a delicious, sweet smell! The boy touched his book, and on it was the pure, rare honey which the angels had gathered from all over the world. He tasted it, and smiled. Eagerly he began to study—at first to find the honey on each page, and then soon to learn the letters, then finally because his study was sweet like honey.

Thus did Simon ben Yehuda receive his reward.

And in time the custom arose of dabbing honey on the pages of each child's first book.

Questions

1 What kind of "learning" is meant in this story?

2 Why do Jews love learning?

3 Why do you think God gave the Torah to Israel?

The Duke of Onions and the Duke of Garlic

7

Introduction

A young prince once had a strange and profitable adventure. When he came home and told about it, his younger brother thought "me too." How do you suppose that worked out?

Story

Long ago a young prince set out to see the world, and to find wisdom. He visited many strange lands and learned many things, until at last he began to miss his own country.

But there was one more place which the prince wanted to visit. And so, on his way home, he stopped at a small, distant island.

The island was much like any other island, except that its people were somewhat backward. To them, left was right, day was night, square was round. Still, they were friendly to the foreign

prince, and their king invited him to a wonderful banquet, in his honor.

That night the prince ate tender roast lamb, and ripe fruit. He drank red wine from the king's vineyards.

"Your Majesty," he said when the meal was over, "I have never eaten such delicious food. Except..."

"Except?!" cried the king. "Except what?!"

"Except that the roast would have tasted better with some onions."

"And what, may I ask, are *onions?*" asked the king.

"Ah," sighed the prince, "onions are the most magical of all foods. Each one has its own pair of green pants, and they stand on their heads, with their legs sticking up in the air. And there is nothing in the world like an onion to bring out the sweet flavor of a good soup, a stew, or a roast."

"If only these remarkable onions grew on our island," said the king. "How I would love to try them!"

"As a matter of fact," said the prince, "my cook has brought onions with him. And tomorrow night, if you like, he will prepare you a banquet."

The next evening the prince's cook made a magnificent feast for the king. There was onion soup, onion bread, roast meat with tender, fried onions. After the meal, the prince gave the king his finest onions, so that the people might plant them, and grow their own crop.

"We must reward you!" cried the king. Then he presented the prince with a heavy sack of silver coins, and a gold-lettered scroll, saying: "Glory to His Majesty, the Duke of Onions!"

Thanking the king, the prince left the island, and sailed home. When he reached his own palace, the entire court gathered round him, begging to hear the story of his adventures. He told them of the island, and showed them the silver, the scroll, and his new title.

Then the prince's younger brother had an idea. "Surely there is more silver on that island," he thought, "and a clever fellow like me should be able to get it."

So he sent three spies to the island, who returned with the news that the backward people there had never tasted garlic. Immediately the young man loaded his ship with garlic, and set sail.

Like his elder brother, the prince was honored with a great banquet. But this time, after dinner, he told the king that the meal would have been much, much better with a little garlic.

"*Garlic?*" asked the king. "Is that anything like *onions?*"

"Garlic is *better* than onions," answered the prince. The next night his cook served a feast, seasoned with garlic. And the prince presented the king with a ship full of garlic.

"You shall be rewarded!" said the king. And he gave the prince a gold-lettered scroll, saying: "Glory to His Majesty, the Duke of Garlic!"

"Is this my whole reward?" asked the disappointed prince, remembering his brother's sack of silver.

"Of course not," said the king. "We will also give you the most precious thing we have."

And, at that moment, the king's servants appeared, bearing the reward—a huge burlap bag, full to the top with large, firm onions!

Questions

1 Are there any old recipes or old customs that your family enjoys very much?

2 If you have something good and have enjoyed it for a long time are you likely to be looking for something new and different?

3 Why do you suppose we Jews value our traditions so highly?

Honi Prays for Rain

8

Introduction

Honi and his neighbors were very practical. They loved God and they felt that God loved them. When they had troubles they did not just shake their heads and sigh. They did something about it.

Story

It happened once in early spring that Honi received a visit from his neighbors.

"The month of Adar is almost over," said an old farmer, pacing back and forth, "and still we have had no rain. Our wells are dry. Our crops cannot grow. Our children have not bathed in thirty days. Please, help us. We know that you are as close to God as a son to his father. Pray to God for rain."

Although he was reluctant, Honi agreed. All day and all night, he prayed for rain. But, in the morning, the sun still shone brightly, and the land was as hot and dry as ever. Honi did not know what to do.

At last he had an idea. He climbed to the top of a rocky, barren hill. He drew a circle in the thick, brown dust. Then Honi planted his feet in the center of the circle, and folded his arms across his chest.

"Master of the Universe!" shouted Honi. "I will not budge from this spot until the dust beneath my feet turns to mud!"

As Honi ended his prayer, a cloud appeared and a light drizzle began to fall from the sky.

The people ran from their homes to see. "Honi," they said, "we are grateful for God's help. But, in truth, this little drizzle is not enough."

"All right," sighed Honi, and began to pray again. "Master of the Universe!" he cried. "Please, be generous with Your rain, for the people need enough water to fill their wells and grow their crops!"

As Honi ended his prayer, the rain increased and the raindrops grew larger—so large, in fact, that each drop was the size of a lake!

The rain kept falling. It struck the earth with loud, hard splashes. Dogs began to bark. Donkeys brayed with fear. Chickens squawked, and flew to the roof of the henhouse.

The water rose so high that the people ran to the hilltop to stay dry.

"Help us!" they cried. "Please, ask God to stop this flood!"

"Master of the Universe!" Honi prayed. "You know that too much is as bad as too little. First the people complained because You sent them no rain. Now they are unhappy because You are sending too much blessing. But they have learned their lesson. And so, I pray You, bring back the sun."

As Honi ended his prayer, a breeze came up and blew away the clouds. The sun shone in the

sky. Now Honi stepped out of his circle. Smiling, the people came down from the hilltop. The children ran to pick the mushrooms which spring up after rain.

From that time forward Honi was known as Honi HaMe'agal, Honi the Circlemaker—because he spoke to God from within the circle as a child speaks to his father.

Questions

1 How did the farmers think about God—to what did they compare him?

2 Why did they ask Honi to pray for them?

3 How long was Honi prepared to talk with God?

Where the Law Is Found

9

Introduction

The garden beside the study house was a peaceful place. A lovely stream ran through it. Here the rabbis would sit discussing the Law and their students would sit to listen. The walls of the study were accustomed to the gentle murmur of serious voices. But then, one day, the rabbis disagreed!

Story

Once it happened that some sages were sitting in a garden beside a study house, discussing a question of law.

Rabbi Eliezer argued one way; but the other sages all disagreed. They discussed the question for many hours, yet still they could not agree. At last, Rabbi Eliezer became angry.

"All right, then," he said. "I will end this argument right now. That carob tree in the corner of the garden will prove that I am right. And then you must all agree."

All at once the tree flew straight into the air,

and landed on the other side of the garden wall!

"That proves nothing," said the other sages. "A flying carob tree has nothing to do with our discussion."

"All right, then," said Rabbi Eliezer. "This lovely stream running through the garden will prove that I am right."

All at once the water in the stream began to flow backward!

"A backward stream proves nothing," said the others.

"If I am right," said Rabbi Eliezer, "let the walls of the study house fall. Then will you agree?"

All at once the walls began to fall!

Frightened, the sages jumped up. But Rabbi Joshua shook his finger at the walls.

"Walls of the academy!" he cried. "Our disagreement is no business of yours! Why must you interfere?"

And the walls stopped falling. Afterward, the walls always leaned, to show their respect for both rabbis.

"I can see that only a voice from heaven will convince you that I am right," said Rabbi Eliezer.

All at once the rabbis heard a heavenly voice!

"Why will you not agree with Rabbi Eliezer?" it asked.

The sages trembled. Rabbi Eliezer smiled. But Rabbi Joshua jumped to his feet.

"No!" he said. "The law is not in heaven!"

"Rabbi Joshua is right," nodded Rabbi Jeremiah. "The Torah was given to us by God. But we are the ones who must interpret it, according to the decision of the majority."

Suddenly, the sun broke through the cloudy sky, and the sages again heard the voice of God.

"My children have overruled me," said the Lord. "But I am pleased, for it means that they are growing up."

Questions

1 Where did the Law come from?

2 Where is it to be used?

3 For practical purposes, how do a group of Jews decide a question when their opinions differ?

4 What attitude did the walls show by continuing to lean a little?

10 The King's Garden

This story of the king's garden is a parable. A parable is a kind of folk tale that tells us a story but is really teaching us about something else.

Story

There once lived a king who had a beautiful garden. In the garden grew bright red roses, and fragrant lilies. Peaches grew the size of melons, and grapes the size of apples.

When it came time to choose a watchman for his garden, the king thought for a long time. He wanted to find a man who would guard the flowers and fruits without being tempted to steal some for himself.

Then, one day, two beggars came to the palace, seeking charity. One was blind, the other lame.

"These are the perfect watchmen for my garden!" said the king. He knew that the blind man could not see the fruit, and that the lame man could not reach even the lowest branches.

45

Delighted by his good fortune, the king paid each of the beggars fifty gold coins, and sent them out to the garden. Hobbling on his crutches, the lame man led his blind friend up and down the shaded paths. And so they began to work.

All day and all night, the two men sat in the garden. Whenever the lame man saw children climbing over the high wall to steal the ripe fruit,

he would tell his partner. Then the blind man would begin to shout until the frightened children ran off.

One morning the blind man turned to his friend. "Why are these children always trying to sneak into the garden?" he asked. "Surely there must be something good to eat here."

"You are right," said the other. "Directly above our heads is a tree loaded with juicy peaches. How I wish I could reach high enough to pick just one!"

"I have an idea," said the blind man. "Why not climb up on my shoulders? Then you could get all the peaches you want."

"But suppose the king catches us?" said his friend.

"He will never catch us," replied the other. "I am blind, and you are lame. The king knows we could never commit such a crime."

Reassured, the lame man climbed up on his friend's shoulders. From then on, the two men helped themselves to all the fruit they desired.

But, one evening, the royal cook came out to pick some peaches for the king's dinner, and discovered there were none left.

When the king heard of this, he became furious, and called the two watchmen to his palace.

"We did nothing wrong!" cried the blind man, trembling before the angry king. "Even if we had such evil thoughts in our minds, our bodies could never have carried them out."

48

The king thought for a long time. At last he realized what had happened. The king ordered the lame man up on the blind man's shoulders. "You were clever partners indeed," said the king. "But as you shared the fruit, now you must share the responsibility. You were like the mind," he said to the lame man. "And you were like the body," he said to the blind one. "The mind and the body are not separate beings."

Then he ordered them both to be punished as one!

Questions

1 How did the lame man and the blind man outwit the king and steal his fruit?

2 To what is the lame man likened? the blind man?

3 Can you do either good or evil without thinking about it first?

The Overcrowded House

11

Introduction

Beryl the farmer was unhappy. So he took his troubles to the rabbi, hoping the rabbi could help him. Surely the wise rabbi would have some good advice, even for a man in Beryl's hard situation.

Story

There once lived a poor farmer named Beryl, who had a very large family, and a very small hut. Now, Beryl's house was so crowded that his ten children had to take turns sleeping in the tiny bed. And, when all were in the hut, someone always had to sit upon the stove.

At last Beryl could stand it no longer. So he went to the village rabbi, and asked him what to do about his overcrowded house.

The wise rabbi thought for a long time. At last he had an idea. "I will tell you what to do," he said. "Bring the chicken inside the house."

Although Beryl wondered how the chicken could help, he trusted the rabbi's wisdom, and did as the rabbi said. But, as soon as the chicken

was inside, it grew frightened, and flew straight at Beryl, knocking him over backward.

So Beryl went back to the rabbi. "The chicken only makes things worse," he said with a sigh.

"In that case," said the rabbi, "I will tell you what to do. Bring in your goat, to live with your family and the chicken."

Still confused, Beryl did as the rabbi said. But, as soon as he brought the goat inside, it began to run around, eating everything in sight. It even ate the feathers which the terrified chicken scattered in the air.

After the goat had eaten Beryl's mattress and the children's clothes, Beryl returned to the rabbi.

"Now, my house is more crowded than ever!" he cried.

"In that case," said the rabbi, "I will tell you what to do. Bring in your cow to live with your family, the chicken, and the goat."

More confused than ever, Beryl went home and brought in the cow. But the huge cow immediately knocked over all the crockery, and nearly stepped into the baby's crib.

Now the house was so crowded that Beryl's children had to press their backs against the wall so that their father could move. And so, squeezing past them, Beryl left the house, and went to the rabbi.

"Rabbi!" he cried. "There is no room to breathe in my house. I am afraid we will all go crazy!"

"Do not worry," said the rabbi. "For I have one more idea. Go home, and take the chicken, the goat, and the cow out of the house. Then see what happens."

Shaking his head, Beryl did as the rabbi said. He put the animals back in the yard. And then he discovered an amazing thing:

Without the animals, the house was as large as a palace! There was room for his children, his wife, and himself!

And so Beryl lived out the rest of his days, happy and content in his big little house.

Questions

1 Why was Beryl unhappy?

2 What advice did the rabbi give him on the first visit? the second? the third?

3 What was the rabbi's last piece of advice, and how did Beryl feel when he had followed it?

4 What really happened? Did the house actually grow larger?

Honor Your Father

12

Introduction

In this story the rabbis learned a lesson from a simple man, named Dima. Most merchants want to make a sale as fast as they can. And they want the highest price possible. But the jeweler, Dima, thought about things differently. He had other values.

Story

One summer forenoon, Dima ben Netina was working in his jewelry shop. As he set precious stones in fine silver, Dima ben Netina whistled happily, but very softly, because he did not want to wake his father, who had fallen fast asleep on a large chest in a corner of the store.

Just before noon, three rabbis entered the shop.

"Welcome," said Dima. "Would you care to see one of these silver rings? Or perhaps you would like a lovely diamond?"

"Thank you," said the eldest rabbi, "but we are here on far more important business. We have heard that you own the largest and most magnificent ruby in the land. We wish to buy it for the

High Priest's breastplate. And we are willing to give you three hundred gold coins."

Dima glanced at the chest in the corner of the store, then he looked back at his customers.

"I am sorry," he said, "but that is impossible."

"All right, then," said the rabbi. "We will give you four hundred."

But Dima ben Netina only smiled sadly, and shook his head.

At this his customers began to scowl. "I see that you are a man who likes to bargain," said the eldest rabbi, "so we will offer you five hundred. But we will go no higher."

"I cannot sell it," said the jeweler.

Then the rabbis began to whisper angrily among themselves. "This jeweler is a thief," they muttered. He wants an outrageous price. Let us offer him six hundred, and let it go at that."

But, when Dima refused to sell the ruby for six hundred, the rabbis grew furious, and began to shout at him.

"You are trying to rob us!" they cried. "How can we pay more than six hundred?"

Before long Dima's father awoke from his nap. He got up from the chest on which he lay, and walked toward the front of the store. "What is the trouble?" he mumbled sleepily.

Dima ben Netina began to smile. He went over to the chest, took out the ruby, and gave it to the rabbis.

"Now you may have it," he said, "for I do not have to wake my father in order to get the jewel. And you must pay me only three hundred gold-pieces, since that is the fair price and it was your first offer."

Smiling happily, the rabbis paid the jeweler, and went back to their study house to tell the story of Dima ben Netina—who respected his father so much that he would not wake him for six hundred pieces of gold.

Questions

1 What Commandment was Dima obeying when he did not go at once to get the ruby?

2 Why did he finally request only the 300 gold pieces for it?

3 How do you think the rabbis felt toward Dima for honoring his father?

13

Someone Sees

Introduction

"The earth is the Lord's, and the fulness thereof" *(Psalms 24:1). Is man, whom God created, ever alone in the world? The driver of the horse-cart thought one thing, the cobbler another.*

Story

One foggy summer afternoon, a cobbler was walking home from a nearby village. He was tired and damp. The muddy earth oozed beneath his feet. And so, when a horsecart passed him on the road, he ran to catch up with it, and asked the driver for a ride.

The driver moved over to make room for him. Chatting pleasantly, the two men continued on their way. But, after a few miles, the driver stopped the cart.

"Look!" he cried, pointing to a tall barn so full of hay that the wooden walls seemed ready to burst. "Surely the lucky man who owns that barn will never notice if my horse helps himself to a good dinner!"

"The farmer does have plenty of hay," agreed the cobbler. "Still he will be angry if he catches you."

"No one will see us in this fog," said the driver. "Besides I have a plan. While my horse eats, we will both stand guard. I will watch the north and east. You look toward the west and south. And, if anyone appears, cry out, *"Someone sees!"* Then we will rush off before they can catch us."

Reluctantly the cobbler agreed. He and the driver took their positions at opposite ends of the cart, and the horse began to eat.

But, before the horse had swallowed two mouthfuls, the cobbler cried out, *"Someone sees!"*

Jumping straight up into the air, the terrified driver raised his whip, and drove away at full speed. He did not slow down until his poor horse was dripping with sweat.

A few minutes later, the driver stopped the cart again. "We are very lucky today," he said. "For there, by the roadside, is a barn full of oats. And perhaps now my horse can eat."

Once again he told the cobbler to cry out if he saw anyone coming. Once again the horse began to eat. And, once again, the cobbler shouted: *"Someone sees!"*

This time the driver jumped even higher than before. He yelled at his horse, and drove furiously down the road.

At last he slowed down, and turned to the cobbler. "I saw no one at all," he began, "who was watching?"

"Someone always sees," replied the cobbler, with a wise smile.

Questions

1 Which of the Ten Commandments was the driver trying to break?

2 Who saw him each time?

3 Have you ever done something wrong when you thought no one was looking? How did you feel later?

14 Who Will Be Zusya?

Introduction

How much does God ask of each of us? Rabbi Zusya had lived a long, good life. He had obeyed the law. Yet he thought about that question as his days drew to a close.

Story

Once there lived a rabbi named Zusya. He was a poor man, who lived among the simple people of his own village. He did not speak like a great scholar, nor did he act like the famous rabbis of the big cities.

But he was a kind, generous man, who followed the commandments of the Torah. And so, many students came to study with Rabbi Zusya, and to learn from the way he lived his life.

Often Rabbi Zusya repeated the same lesson. "Listen to your own heart," he told his students. "And try to live as the still, small voice inside you tells you."

Then the rabbi's students would nod with understanding, and would ask God to help them hear the voice of their own hearts.

One day, Rabbi Zusya failed to arrive at the study house. His students waited and waited, yet their teacher did not come. At last they become worried, and rushed to the rabbi's house.

There they discovered a terrible thing. The rabbi was sick, too ill to move. He lay on his bed, trembling, with the blankets pulled up over his shoulders.

"I am dying," said Rabbi Zusya. "And I am very frightened."

"Why are you afraid?" asked the rabbi's favorite student. "Surely you cannot be worried that God will find fault with you. All your life, you kept the commandments as faithfully as Moses. All your life, you prayed as steadily as Abraham. Why, then, should you fear to face the Lord?"

"That is not what frightens me," replied Rabbi Zusya, "for, if the Lord asks me why I did not act like Moses, I can tell Him that I was not Moses. If the Lord asks me why I did not act like Abraham, I can tell him that I was not Abraham.

"But, when the Lord says, 'Zusya, how can you account for those times when you did not act like Zusya—what can I tell Him then?"

And so, even at the moment of his death, Rabbi Zusya taught his students to be true to their own hearts—their own natures.

Questions

1 Can anyone expect to take another's place in life?

2 What is the very best that God expects of each of us?

3 Do you think anyone succeeds in being his own best self all the time? Does it help to try?

15 Seven Years of Plenty

Introduction

"Jam yesterday, and jam tomorrow, but never jam today." Have you ever heard that saying? "Jam," of course, stands for anything good that we might like to have. And sometimes we want our jam NOW.

Story

A poor farmer was hard at work, plowing his land. Just before noon, he looked up from his work, and saw an old Arab in a red silk turban walking across the fields.

"What are you doing here?" demanded the farmer.

"I have come from God to offer you seven years of plenty," replied the Arab.

"You have come from the devil to tease me about my poverty," cried the farmer.

"God has granted you seven years of plenty," the Arab repeated patiently. "You may have them right away. Or, you may wait until later, and live seven comfortable years in your old age. The choice is up to you."

"I suppose I have nothing to lose," said the farmer. "But please, wait a moment, so I may go home and ask my wife's advice."

The farmer began to run. He ran down the road to his hut. He ran through the courtyard, where his children were digging in the dirt. He ran straight to the kitchen, where his plump, cheerful wife was baking bread for lunch.

Breathless from running, the farmer told her what had happened.

"Run right back," she told him, "and tell the Arab that we would like our seven years to begin at once."

The farmer did as his wife said. And that night, he returned to find his hut full of treasure. Stacks of shining gold coins reached the ceiling. The

tables were covered with emeralds and rubies. Even the soup bowls were full of silver and diamonds.

"Father!" cried the farmer's children. "Look what we found this afternoon, digging in the courtyard!"

That night the family ate roast chicken and wine. But, after dinner, the farmer began to sigh.

"We will need this comfort even more in our old age," he said. "Perhaps we should have waited."

"Do not worry," smiled his wife. "We will try to spend our fortune wisely."

The next morning the farmer's wife took ten of her new gold coins, and bought food for all the beggars in the marketplace.

Soon she and her husband became famous for their charity. They gave money to widows and orphans, bought books for penniless students. Poor men traveled from all over to eat at the farmer's table.

In this way, seven years passed.

Then, one morning, the old Arab in the red silk turban appeared at the farmer's door.

"I remember you," said the farmer sadly.

"Good," said the Arab. "For I am here to collect the money God gave you, seven years ago."

Just then the farmer's wife stepped forward. "I will make you a bargain," she told the Arab. "If you can find two people more charitable, we will give back the money at once.

"Certainly, you must agree, we did not use the gold only for ourselves. No, we acted as though God had entrusted the money to us to do all the good deeds which please Him."

The Arab shut his eyes, as if he were listening to a distant voice. Then he opened them again.

"Now I will tell you who I really am," he said. "I am Elijah, the Prophet, and I travel the world in many disguises, doing God's will. But you are right—never, in all my travels, have I met such a charitable couple.

"God will let you keep the wealth," smiled Elijah. "And He will give you a long, happy life, as a reward for your generosity and righteousness."

Questions

1 Who was the "Arab" really?

2 Do you think the couple made the right choice?

3 How did they use the wealth, and why were they allowed to keep it?

David and the Spider

16

Introduction

You know how David killed the giant, Goliath. Young David had many other adventures, too, before he became the King of Israel. And sometimes David had some very narrow escapes.

Story

Once, in the days before he became king, David was walking in the woods. He noticed a spider spinning its web between two twigs and stopped to watch how carefully it worked.

After a while, a storm came up, and a strong wind ripped the spider's perfect, delicate web to shreds.

"What a waste!" thought David. "Why did God bother to create this creature which wastes all its time spinning a useless web?"

The storm grew fiercer. Thunder began to roar. Suddenly, David saw someone running toward him, through the rain.

It was his best friend, Jonathan, the son of King Saul.

70

"David!" cried Jonathan. "You must escape right away. My father, the King, is jealous of you because the people love you so much. He is afraid that you will try to steal his throne. And he has ordered his armies to find you, and kill you. Run away, run as fast as you can!"

David thanked his friend and fled.

He ran through the wet forest, down from the mountains. He ran south, into the desert. Often Saul's soldiers drew so close that David could see them over his shoulder. But always, he managed to escape.

At last he reached the wilderness of En Gedi. He knew that the army was only a few miles behind him. He was terrified, worn out. There was nowhere to hide.

Then he saw a small cave in a rock. He crawled inside and waited. An hour later, he heard the hoofbeats of the army's horses. He heard the soldiers stop in front of the cave and walk up to the entrance.

"Now they have found me," sighed David.

But—much to his surprise—the soldiers came no further!

"He cannot be hiding in there," David heard them shouting as they rode away. "He would have broken that huge spiderweb across the mouth of the cave. No one has been in there for months!"

David looked, and saw that it was true. While he was hiding, a spider had spun its delicate web across the mouth of the cave. The spider had saved his life!

"Now I understand!" cried David. "Every one of God's creatures—even this little spider—is precious. Every one of them has its purpose in the world!"

Questions

1 Why did David have to flee for his life?

2 How did his best friend help him?

3 What other creature helped him, and what did David learn from this?

Moses and the Lost Lamb

17

Introduction

Moses was a shepherd before he became the great leader of the Exodus. We can see him here, doing the daily tasks that fall to any shepherd.

Story

When Moses was a young man, he spent his days as a shepherd, caring for his father-in-law's flocks in the land of Midian.

One summer afternoon, as Moses was guiding the herd through a sweet green pasture, he counted the sheep, and found one missing. "Perhaps I have made a mistake," he thought, and counted again. Yet no matter how many times he counted, the total remained the same: One of the animals was gone.

At that moment, Moses glanced out of the corner of his eye, and noticed the smallest lamb in the flock, disappearing behind a rise at the edge of the field. Leaving his dog to watch the

76

grazing herd, Moses threw down his staff, and ran after the lamb.

For almost an hour, he pursued the tiny animal through the tall, soft grass, through the thick woods, across the slippery marshes. The lamb's spindly legs trembled and shook, yet still it managed to elude the strong young shepherd.

"What could have gotten into the creature?" wondered Moses, panting from the effort of the chase. "Did something frighten it? Why does it want to escape?"

It was not until Moses reached the crest of a pleasant, shaded valley that he began to understand. There, just below him, the lamb had stopped on the banks of a cool, bubbling stream, and was eagerly lapping up the water, as if it had not touched a drop of moisture in weeks.

"Now I see," said Moses. "Drink little lamb, and be satisfied."

Although the sun had begun to set, Moses waited patiently until the lamb finished drinking. Then, walking softly to keep from startling it, he crept down the side of the valley, and lifted the runaway into his arms.

Holding the lamb tenderly against his chest, Moses murmured and sang to calm it. He did not stop walking until he had returned to the sheep meadow. Gently he placed the lamb near its mother's side.

And it was then that God was heard.

"Just as the lamb was thirsty for water," said the Lord, "so my people Israel are thirsty for their freedom. And just as Moses led the lamb back from the water—with the same understanding and compassion shall Moses lead my people into the Promised Land."

Questions

1 What did the runaway lamb want so badly?

2 What did the Hebrew people want?

3 What qualities shown by Moses would be needed in the great work that lay before him?

A Wife for Isaac

18

Introduction

The worship of the One God began with Abraham. It was to be carried on by Abraham's son Isaac, and by Isaac's sons' sons, and so on and on. But the survival of the Jewish faith has always depended on women as well as on men. You can see it was most important that Isaac find just the right sort of wife.

Story

Long ago, Abraham decided that it was time for his son to marry. So he told his most trusted servant, Eliezer, "Go to the city where my brother Nahor, lives to seek out a wife for my son, Isaac."

"But how will I know her?" asked the aged servant. "Will she be tall or short, dark or fair? Tell me, at least, what sort of woman Isaac would like."

"God will point her out to you," replied Abraham, and sent Eliezer on his way.

Eliezer saddled ten of Abraham's camels, loaded them with gifts and spices, and set out across the desert. He reached the city of Nahor at twilight,

and led his camels to the village well. There he saw many young women, laughing and talking as they filled their water-jars.

"So many women!" thought Eliezer. "How will I choose the right one?" But he remembered Abraham's words, and began to pray.

"Lord," he prayed, "please, help me find a good wife for Isaac."

At that moment, he noticed a beautiful young woman, standing beside the well. On her shoulder was a brown clay pitcher, full of cold, fresh water.

Bowing politely, Eliezer approached her. "I am a stranger here," he said. "I have traveled many miles across the desert. Now, I am very thirsty. May I please drink some water from your jar?"

"Yes, my Lord," replied the young woman.

The old man drank gratefully, emptying half the pitcher in three huge gulps. But, before he could thank the woman, she spoke again.

"Your camels must also be thirsty," she said. "They, too, have felt the hot desert sun."

She went to the well, and drew more water. Refilling and emptying her pitcher, she carried water to the camels until all the animals were satisfied.

"What is your name?" asked the servant.

"I am Rebekah, the daughter of Bethuel," she said.

"And is there room in your father's house for a tired traveler to sleep?" he asked.

"Yes," said Rebekah, and led Eliezer to her home, where he dined on fresh bread and mutton.

After the meal, old Eliezer began to praise his master, Abraham's son. "Isaac is just the husband for Rebekah," he told the young woman's family.

Rebekah listened silently, for a long time. At last, when the servant spoke of Isaac's great wisdom and generosity, she nodded her head in agreement.

Then, Abraham's servant smiled. And he made gifts of many jewels and rare spices to Rebekah and her family. And he thanked God for helping him find the kind Rebekah for Isaac.

Questions

1 We know that Abraham had always trusted God. Would you expect his servant Eliezer to do the same?

2 What good qualities did Rebekah show in her reply to Eliezer?

3 What value does Jewish teaching place on these qualities?

19

Introduction

King Solomon had been blessed by God with wisdom, honor, and riches. But according to this legend, even Solomon sometimes forgot something important and had to learn it anew.

Story

One night, a foreign ambassador visited King Solomon's palace. The king served him a lavish feast. But, feeling very tired that evening, Solomon treated his guest coldly, and hardly spoke to him.

After dinner, the ambassador frowned. "Tomorrow, we will discuss important matters," he said.

"Of course," nodded Solomon, and went off to his royal bedchamber to sleep.

But the next morning, when Solomon awoke, he was no longer in his room, or in his palace. He was lying in the gutter of the marketplace! Overnight, the king had been turned into a beggar!

Dirty, tattered rags covered his body. His beard

was matted and greasy. And soon his stomach felt empty.

At twilight a rich merchant was hurrying through the marketplace. Now this merchant rarely noticed beggars. But, on that day, he tripped on a stone, and quickly looked to see if anyone was watching.

The merchant saw a filthy old man at his feet. And suddenly he recognized the beggar as King Solomon!

"Your Majesty!" he cried. "What tragedy has brought you to such a miserable state?"

"I am not sure," sighed the king. "Perhaps I am being taught a lesson, though I do not yet know what it is."

"In that case," smiled the merchant, "*I* will give the banquet tonight. Come home and dine with me, so that I may have the King of Israel as my guest."

Solomon eagerly followed the merchant to his mansion. As soon as they entered the dining room, servants brought in platters of roast lamb, pitchers of wine, and bowls of raisins, fruit, and almonds.

"My only regret," said the merchant, as he piled food on his plate, "is that this feast seems so meager compared to the wonderful feasts *you* used to give. Does it not sadden you, my poor

king, to think that you will never give such glorious banquets again? It must be terrible to know that you will be poor and unhappy for the rest of your life!"

The merchant went on in this way until Solomon's throat was so choked with tears that he could hardly swallow. "I suppose I am not as hungry as I thought," he said sadly, and left the merchant's house.

The next morning King Solomon awoke in the gutter, dirtier and hungrier than before. Once again he could find nothing to eat all day. He stared hungrily at the vegetables, hoping that some charitable housewife would give him a few fresh greens.

That evening he met a thin, old man, carrying a sack of onions on his back. Now the onion-seller was a poor man, but, each night, he wandered through the market until he found a beggar to share his simple meal.

He led the king to a thatched hut, where he served him a bowl of thin onion soup. And only then did he ask his guest's name.

Reluctantly Solomon told his story. But, unlike the merchant, the onion-seller broke into a broad grin.

"Then there is no reason to worry!" he cried. "You yourself know what God has promised—King David's descendants will always rule our kingdom. Surely you will be king again—it is only a matter of time!"

Smiling happily, the king drank the small bowl of soup, then thanked his host.

"I am sorry for the plainness of the meal," said the poor man. "But I can only afford what I bring home from the stall."

Then it was Solomon's turn to grin. "I cannot thank you enough," he said, "for you have taught me more than you know. Listen: two nights ago, an angel came to my palace, disguised as a foreign ambassador. I treated him coldly, so God put me out on the streets, to learn this lesson:

"Yesterday evening, I dined on meat and wine, but the food was seasoned with unkindness, and tasted as bitter as ashes. But tonight this thin soup seemed sweeter to me than the finest raisins and almonds in all Israel, because it was seasoned with generosity and with love."

Questions

1 What did King Solomon need to remember about hospitality?

2 Why couldn't the king enjoy the rich merchant's fine dinner?

3 What "seasoning" made the onion-seller's soup taste so good to the king?

4 How is this story like "The Sabbath Spice"?

20

Two Puddings

Introduction

The maggid of Koznitz saw many troubled people who came to ask his advice. But two of the strangest he ever saw were the couple who quarreled about pudding.

Story

One day the maggid of Koznitz looked out his window to see a fat man and his fat wife approaching his house. They were joking merrily as they walked. The man's great stomach shook with laughter. His wife was so huge that she could not see the ground beneath her feet. And so, whenever she stumbled on the potholes in the roadway, her husband gently reached out to guide her.

"Look at that nice couple!" said the maggid to his wife. "Surely they are not the sort of people who usually ask me for advice. Surely they will not burden me with some awful tale of trouble and woe."

But as soon as the couple entered the maggid's parlor, and squeezed their enormous bodies onto the tiny sofa, their faces grew long and sad.

"Our marriage is over," sighed the man.

"But why?" asked the maggid. "You seem so happy."

"The problem is with the pudding," said the woman, looking sadly at the floor. "We cannot agree about the pudding."

"The pudding?" asked the maggid, surprised.

"Yes," nodded the man. "My wife is a wonderful cook," he explained. "Every Friday night, she prepares me a delicious meal of fresh fish, crisp roast chicken, tasty yams, and tender carrots. And, at the end of the dinner, she brings in the best dish of all—a beautiful, steaming, golden-brown pudding, which has a sweeter aroma than anything on earth."

"Then you are a very lucky husband," smiled the maggid.

"Not at all," said the man, sighing again, "Because, by the time I have eaten that fine meal, I never have enough room left for the pudding. So I must sit there, staring at it, feeling terribly sad."

90

"Then perhaps your wife should serve the pudding at the start of the meal," said the maggid quickly.

"That is just what my husband says," answered the woman. "And that is the beginning of all our arguments. I cannot agree, because, long ago, my mother taught me that the pudding should always be served last. And now, no matter how I try, I cannot bring myself to go against that custom."

"It is a pity," nodded her husband. "My wife and I want very much to stay together. But, unless this pudding problem is solved, we cannot go on."

"Perhaps I can find a solution," said the maggid. "Let me think." He fell silent for a long time. Then he smiled.

"I have an idea," he told the woman at last. "Why not make *two* puddings? You could serve one at the end of the meal, just as your mother taught. And you could serve the other at the beginning, so your husband could eat it. Is that not the perfect answer?"

The fat man and his wife broke into broad, happy grins, and hugged each other joyously. "Let us go home," said the woman, taking her husband by the arm. "I will start baking immediately."

Thanking the maggid, the couple hurried out the door. At that moment, the maggid's wife returned to the parlor. "Look at the smile on your face!" she said to her husband. "Usually, when people come asking you for advice, you frown for days."

"This time I am cheerful," answered the maggid, "because that couple came to me not in anger and despair, but in love and hope. They honestly wanted a good solution to their problem. They were delighted when I found them one!"

Questions

1 What was the couple's quarrel about pudding?

2 How did the maggid solve it?

3 In what spirit had these two people come to see the maggid, and how did that help?

21

The Fishing Lesson

Introduction

The tradition teaches us to love our neighbor as ourselves. And there is a saying, "To love is to give." Still, there are ways and ways of giving, as you will see in "The Fishing Lesson."

Story

Many years ago there lived two fishermen, Simon and Jacob. Simon was an old man, Jacob was quite young. Still, they loved to work together, and learned many things from each other.

One sunny morning the two fishermen stood on the banks of a clear river, casting their lines into the rushing water. After a while they noticed a skinny beggar, coming out of the forest.

The beggar's torn clothes were covered with thistles. His feet were black with mud. So many leaves were stuck in his hair that he looked like a small, skinny tree.

"Gentlemen," said the beggar, addressing the fisherman, "I see that you are having a lucky morning. You have caught a basket of trout, a bucketful of salmon. Those two kettles are overflowing with bass. Surely you can spare a few fish for a hungry, hungry beggar like myself."

Jacob, who felt sorry for the beggar, quickly reached into the basket, and pulled out the biggest trout. But, before he could give the fish away, Simon stopped him.

"We have no fish to spare," Simon told the beggar, "but come stand next to me, and I will show you how to catch your own."

The beggar hesitated a moment, then joined Simon at the water's edge. Patiently, Simon showed the poor man how to make a fishing pole and line from a long stick, a hook, and some string. He showed him how to use a worm as bait, and how to cast his line far into the water.

At first the beggar had no success, and he began to mutter angrily. But, at last, he felt a tug on his line, and pulled a fat, rainbow-colored bass out of the water.

Grinning happily, the beggar stuffed the fish into the front of his shirt, and went off to cook his lunch.

After he was gone, Jacob turned to Simon. "I am surprised at you," he said. "Have you no heart? Why did you stop me from giving that hungry man a fish as soon as he asked for it?"

"Jacob," Simon replied, "if you had given the beggar a fish, he would have eaten it quickly. He would be hungry again by tonight. But, by teaching him how to catch his own fish, I showed him how to get food for the rest of his life. And he will never go hungry again."

Questions

1 What did the poor beggar ask for?

2 Which would have been the easier and quicker way of helping him, Simon's way or Jacob's?

3 Which was the more valuable—the better—way in the long run?

The First Farmer

22

Introduction

The Garden of Eden was a place of wonder and delight. Yet the Bible tells us that God put Adam there "to till it and look after it."

Story

Long, long ago, before God created Adam, He made the Garden of Eden as beautiful as could be, to welcome the first man.

The Lord loaded the trees with ripe, heavy fruit. He dusted the grass with tiny drops of dew. He dressed the peacocks in their brightest finery so that their feathers gleamed in the sun.

When Adam opened his eyes, he rejoiced to see his magnificent home.

"All that I have created, for you have I created," the Lord said. "If you do not keep it well, no one after you will be able to set it right."

Adam lived happily in his new home. Each day he explored the garden, marveling at its beauty. He smelled the sweet flowers and tasted the ripe fruit. He felt the soft grass beneath his feet. He watched the peacocks show their feathers and the goldfish swim in the clear lakes. And he laughed at the antics of the monkeys, as they climbed the trees and threw oranges down at the ground.

Each night, before he went to sleep, Adam thanked God for giving him such a wonderful place to live.

But, one morning, Adam awoke to find everything changed. Something terrible had happened! The grass was dry and brown. The fruits were shrunken, and full of worms. The flowers drooped sadly on their stems. And the peacocks' feathers seemed dull and thin.

Adam could not understand what had happened. Hoping that a little food might make him think more clearly, he picked some fruit from a peach tree. But the peaches were covered with brown, rotten spots, and tasted bitter in his mouth.

As the days passed, the garden grew worse. The plants were all dying. The animals were too weak from hunger to run and play. Adam was hungry for the first time in his life, and he became frightened.

So he prayed to God. "Lord of the Universe," he prayed. "Please, tell me why this terrible thing is happening to my home."

Then God answered Adam's prayer.

"Adam," said the Lord, "your home will not stay beautiful unless you take care of it. There is much work for you to do here."

"I will do anything!" cried Adam. "Just show me what is needed!"

The next morning, when Adam awoke, God showed him how to care for the garden. He taught Adam how to water the grass, and how to pull the weeds from among the flowers. He taught Adam how to trim the dead branches from the fruit trees so that they could get enough light. And he taught Adam how to feed the peacocks so that their feathers would always shine brightly.

And that is how Adam became the first farmer.

Questions

1 Was Adam doing his full part when he just thanked God for the garden?

2 What else was required of Adam?

3 In what ways are we all "partners with God" in caring for our world and helping to make it a better place?

100

23 The King and the Awl

Introduction

"He cares only for himself." That is a bad thing for anyone to have to say of another, but you may have heard it. And it was certainly true of the selfish king in this story. The king had some "waking up" to do!

Story

Once there lived a king so selfish, that whenever he saw a child eating pastry, he would snatch the cake away, and gobble it down himself.

He took all the grain in his kingdom, and stored it in his storehouses. He took all the gold, and locked it in his treasury. He took all the food, and put it away in his huge pantry.

At last he took so much that the people in his kingdom had nothing left to eat. Starving with hunger, they decided to ask the king for help. But they were all so frightened of the selfish king that no one dared approach him.

Finally a wrinkled fisherman came forward. "I am very old," he said. "I have had a good life. Even if the king hangs me, I have little left to lose."

So the old fisherman went to the royal palace, and asked the king to give the people food.

"I am sorry that my subjects are starving," said the king, yawning idly. "But that is not my concern. Their bellies are not the same as mine. I cannot feel their hunger pains. Why should I trouble myself with their problems?"

"You are right, Your Majesty," nodded the fisherman. "And, just to prove that I have no hard feelings, I will do you a favor:

"I know a place where thousands of bright, rainbow-colored fish live just beneath the surface of the sea. I also know how much Your Majesty

loves beautiful things. I will take you there, and perhaps you can bring back a few orange and purple fish to keep in the moat."

This idea pleased the selfish king so much that he immediately followed the fisherman to his boat. He sat in the tiny boat and sunned himself while the old man rowed away from shore.

They stopped in the middle of the ocean. Water surrounded them, as far as the king could see.

Eager to behold the wondrous fish, the king leaned over the side of the boat. But, when he saw that there was nothing in the water but seaweed, he looked back at the fisherman.

He was amazed to see the fisherman chipping away at the bottom of the boat with a large awl!

"What are you doing?" cried the king, as water trickled into the boat. "Is that how you catch fish?"

"No, I am sinking the boat," explained the fisherman. "I am so hungry that I want to die. And now seems as good a time as any."

"But *I* do not want to die." cried the king.

"I know," said the fisherman. "That is why I am only going to make the hole in my end of the boat. What happens at your end of the boat is not my concern."

Forgetting his terror, the king laughed. "I see what you are trying to tell me," he said. "Now, row back to shore, and I will use my storehouses of grain to feed all the people in the kingdom."

Questions

1 Why were the king's subjects so unhappy?

2 How did the fisherman persuade the king to go fishing with him?

3 How did his drilling a hole in the boat teach the king a lesson?

24

Come In, and Close the Door

Introduction

Shloime and his wife had "I" trouble. In fact, they had quite bad cases of it, as you will see.

Story

One cold winter night, as Shloime and his wife slept in their bed they were awakened by a loud noise and a gust of icy air.

"The wind has blown the door open," Shloime told his wife. "Get up, and close it."

"*You* close it," muttered the sleepy woman.

"No," insisted Shloime. "I have already told you to do it. And I never back down on my word."

"Neither do I," said his wife proudly. "And *I* am not going to close that door."

"All right, then," said Shloime. "I can see that we are never going to agree. So let us make a bargain: Whoever speaks first must get up and close the door."

Shloime's wife put her finger against her lips and nodded. Then she pulled the blankets over her head. The stubborn couple lay there silently, shivering, listening to the slamming and creaking of their door. Each one waited for the other to say the first word.

Suddenly they heard the sound of heavy footsteps in the front room. "How lucky of us to find an open door!" said a gruff-voiced man. "These careless people deserve to have everything in their house stolen!"

Trembling with fear, Shloime's wife heard the clatter of silverware and copper kettles, as the thieves filled their sacks. Shloime listened to them take all his precious books down from the shelves, and carry them out the open door.

But still the couple kept silent.

Finally, at dawn, they got out of bed and went into the front room. There they saw that nothing was left but a few pieces of heavy furniture. The thieves had stolen everything they could carry!

"Perhaps we will feel better after breakfast," thought the unhappy woman. But the pots and pans were missing from the shelves, and there was nothing to eat in the pantry. Pointing at her stomach, Shloime's wife went off to borrow some food from a neighbor.

While she was gone, Shloime prepared to go to the synagogue. But the thieves had stolen his prayerbooks! So he sat in his chair, and shivered in the cold draft.

Just then, a traveling barber walked through the open door. "I see that you need a haircut!" he told Shloime. And, when Shloime said nothing, the barber took it as a sign of agreement, and took out his scissors and combs.

"Tell me when to stop," said the barber, snipping steadily at Shloime's hair and beard. But, of course, the stubborn man said nothing.

By the time the barber finished, Shloime was as bald as a plucked chicken, and nothing was left of his beard but three gray hairs.

"Now pay me," said the barber. But Shloime still kept silent, and the barber grew furious. "I'll teach you not to pay me!" he said. He grabbed a big handful of grease and soot from the stove, and rubbed it all over Shloime's face. Then he stalked out through the open door.

A moment later, Shloime's wife came home. She took one look at her hairless, greasy, sooty husband, and began to scream. "Shloime!" she cried. "What happened?!"

Shloime smiled and shrugged his shoulders. "So," he said, in a warm, gentle voice. "You have spoken the first word. Now please, come in, and close the door."

Questions

1 How early in the story does the "I" problem appear?

2 What hardships came upon these two people because each was so self-willed and stubborn?

3 Aside from their stubbornness, did it really much matter which of them closed the door?

The Goat that Made the Stars Sing

Introduction

When the world was very new "the morning stars sang together" (Job 38:7). They don't sing anymore. This legend tells us how the stars once sang—and why they stopped.

Story

Once there was a goat with horns so long that they reached the sky. Each night, he would gently brush the heavens with his horns. As he touched the stars, they began to sing. And, each night, the people were lulled to sleep by the mystical, beautiful music of the stars.

One day, as the goat was grazing in a field, he saw a young man, angrily kicking stones in the road. "What is the matter?" asked the goat.

"I am terribly unhappy," replied the man. "I have just lost my snuffbox, and now I cannot carry my tobacco with me from place to place. What shall I do?"

But seeing the goat, the man had an idea. "Pardon me," he said politely. "Could I take a

little bit of your horn, so that I could use it to carve myself a new snuffbox?"

"Of course," replied the goat kindly, and lowered his horns until they touched the ground.

The man took hold of one horn. He knew that these were the wonderful horns which made the stars sing. But right now, he wanted a snuffbox for his tobacco. So he quickly cut off a bit of horn and ran home.

As soon as the man finished carving his snuffbox, he showed it to his friends. "What a beautiful snuffbox!" cried the villagers. "Where did you get it?"

When the man told them about the goat, they all became excited. "Every one of us can have his own snuffbox!" they cried. "Let us go find the goat!"

At this, a little girl, who was standing nearby, grew worried. "If you cut any more from the goat's horns," she said, "they will be too short to reach the sky. And the stars will not sing any more."

"Do not worry," the villagers told her, "each of us will take only a small piece. Besides we must have our snuffboxes."

They rushed off to look for the magical goat. When they found him, they crowded around, each begging for a bit of horn.

The goat, who was too kind to refuse, meekly lowered his head. One by one, each villager cut off a portion. No one cared that the horns were indeed growing shorter and shorter.

That night, the stars did not sing. For the sad goat could not brush the sky with his shortened horns, no matter how hard he tried.

Questions

1 Why could the poor goat no longer make the stars sing?

2 Did it help matters at all that each single person was only a little bit to blame?

3 Why couldn't the people have listened to the little girl who warned them?

The Betrayal of the Trees

26

Introduction

The trees were warned that they should be loyal to one another. And most of them remembered —most of them.

Story

On the third day of Creation, God made the trees. He created the tall pine, the beautiful elm, and the rich, dark redwood. And the trees stood on the earth, and greeted each other by shaking their bright leaves in the wind.

But, on that same day, God made the metals. He made the shining silver, the gold, and the red copper. And he created the dark iron, hidden deep beneath the ground.

When the trees heard about the creation of iron, they became frightened. The birches and the aspens began to tremble. And the trees cried out to God.

"Please Lord," cried the cedar. "Why did you make the iron? Now men will be able to make axe blades and chop us down."

114

"Do not worry," said the Lord. "I did not create the iron to harm you. The iron alone cannot cut you down, for men cannot make an axe without wood for the handle. If you live together in harmony, without betraying one another, there will be no wood for the handle, and no axe."

So the trees grew calm again. But the iron, who was listening to all this very carefully, found a clever plan. He went to the base of a tall oak, and began to talk in his harsh, rasping voice.

"Oak!" he said. "Why is a fine tree like you wasting his time in this forest? You are hidden here, no one notices you. God made you for better things. Give me a handle for my blade, come with me, and together we will build great cities."

For a moment, the oak remembered God's warning, and hesitated. But he wanted the fame and glory which the iron promised. And so, at last, he agreed.

Together the iron and the oak made an axe. Soon men came into the forest, and began to chop down the trees. One by one, the tall trees cried out, and fell to the ground.

At last the woodcutters reached the oak which had given the wood for the axe handle.

"No!" cried the oak. "Do not cut *me* down! I am on your side. You would not even have an axe if not for me!"

But the woodsmen did not hear, and raised their axes higher. So the oak began to plead with the iron blade.

"Remember me?" asked the oak. "I am your partner!"

"I cannot remember a thing," said the iron blade, as it bit into the frightened oak.

"I am sorry I ever listened to you!" cried the oak. Then it crashed heavily to the ground.

And so it happened that the trees of the forest were betrayed by one of their own.

Questions

1 Why was it important for the trees to live together in harmony?

2 How did the iron persuade the oak to betray the other trees?

3 How many people does it take to cause trouble for a lot of others?

Samuel's Call

27

Introduction

Samuel's mother and father, Hannah and Elkanah, had no children. Hannah prayed to be given a son so when her baby was born, she named him Samuel to show she had "asked him of the Lord." She was so grateful to have the little boy that she brought him to live in the Temple and serve God.

Story

When Samuel was a boy, he lived with his teacher, Eli, in the temple at Shiloh.

Samuel and Eli loved each other very much. Although Eli was very old, Samuel knew that he was still young in spirit, and that his years had given him great wisdom. Although Eli's eyes were weak with age, Samuel knew that he often saw deep into men's souls. Eli understood things which seemed mysterious to the boy.

All day long, Samuel sat in the temple courtyard, listening to Eli speak of God, the Torah, justice, charity, and kindness. When night came, Samuel was always disappointed, and begged Eli to teach him a little more before it was time to sleep. Then Eli would laugh gently, and reach out to touch his student's eager young face.

One night, as Samuel lay half-asleep in his tiny room, he heard a soft voice calling his name.

"It is Eli," he thought. "Perhaps he has some thing more to teach me." Leaping out of bed, Samuel rushed to his teacher's room.

"Why did you call me?" he asked the old man.

"I did not call you," replied Eli, sleepily. "Go back to bed."

So Samuel returned to his own room. But, as soon as he lay down, he heard the voice again. "Samuel." It called so quietly that the boy wondered if perhaps he was imagining it.

Still he ran again to Eli's room.

"You are dreaming again," laughed Eli. "Go back, and may the Lord permit you to sleep more soundly."

So Samuel did as Eli said. But, as soon as he lay down on his bed, the voice called him again. "Samuel!" it called. And, this time, he knew that he was not dreaming.

He went to his teacher's room once more. "Eli," he said, "I am frightened. Someone has called me three times. Are you *sure* it was not you?"

"No, I did not call you," said Eli, reaching out to comfort the troubled boy. As he touched Samuel's face, the old man began to understand.

"Now it is clear to me," said Eli. "It was God who called you. You must listen carefully to His voice, Samuel. You must do as He tells you. And you must deliver His word to His people. When you are troubled, and His voice seems too quiet to hear, you must listen closely, and you will hear His message."

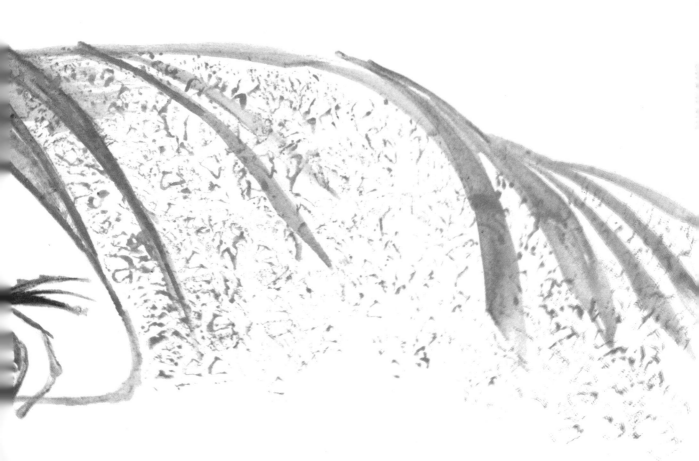

Samuel thanked his teacher. He went back to his room, and lay down on his bed. But, this time, he was ready, listening very carefully, to answer the voice which speaks in silence.

Questions

1 Who did Samuel think had called him?

2 Who had really called him?

3 How had Samuel been prepared to hear that call?

28 The Silence

Introduction

The Psalmist sang, "Be still and know that I am God" (Psalms 46:11). This story tells of a deep deep stillness, long ago.

Story

One bright summer morning, Rabbi Yohanan's students sat in their study house, talking softly as they waited for their teacher to start the lesson. When at last the rabbi walked to the center of the room, he had to wait several minutes for his students to grow quiet. Then he began:

Once there was a single moment when the whole world was perfectly silent. Birds did not sing or flap their wings. The cows stopped munching their fodder, and the sheep perked up their ears to listen. Oxen would not pull the plows through the fields, but waited quietly. Even the youngest babies stopped laughing and playing.

The silence spread across the face of the earth, from the east to the west, from the north to the south. Not a single creature stirred.

Standing at the foot of Mount Sinai, the Jewish people could almost hear the sound of their own hearts beating.

Then, from deep inside the most secret places of the silence, came a still, small voice:

1 I am the Lord your God who brought you out of Egypt. You shall have no other gods beside Me.

2 You shall not make any idols, or worship them.

3 You shall not swear falsely by My name.

4 Remember the Sabbath day and keep it holy.

5 Honor your father and your mother.

6 You shall not murder.

7 You shall not commit adultery.

8 You shall not steal.

9 You shall not bear false witness against your neighbor.

10 You shall not be envious, or want for yourself anything that belongs to your neighbor.

All the creatures on earth listened to the soft voice; they held their breath, and were silent. And, because the commandments were spoken in the deep silence, they became a part of the silence within our own hearts.

And, if we can only learn to listen quietly enough, we can still hear the echoes of that voice that spoke in the silence.

127

So saying, Rabbi Yohanan stopped speaking and began to pray. And all of his students in the study house began to pray silently, and to listen carefully.

Questions

1 What great Commandments were given in the silence?

2 What was the "still, small voice" that gave them?

3 Why do we sometimes pray and listen in silence today?